HUGS OF ARGYLL

Huggy's Big Day

Caeleigh Kean

HUGS OF ARGYLL

For my daughter, Haileigh

Huggy was not just an ordinary pony; he had a very special job. He was a therapist who provided therapy to

Children

Teenagers

and adults

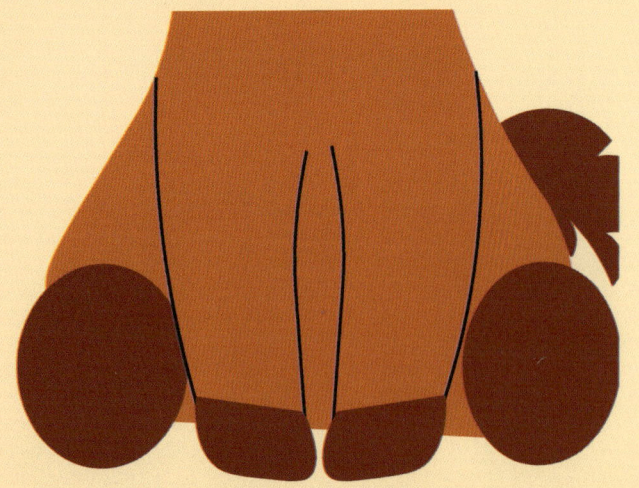

Huggy had a soft and fluffy chestnut coat,

big round eyes,

and a warm smile that could brighten anyone's day.

He lived in a cozy stable with his best friends..

One sunny morning, as Huggy trotted through the village, and noticed a group of children playing in the park

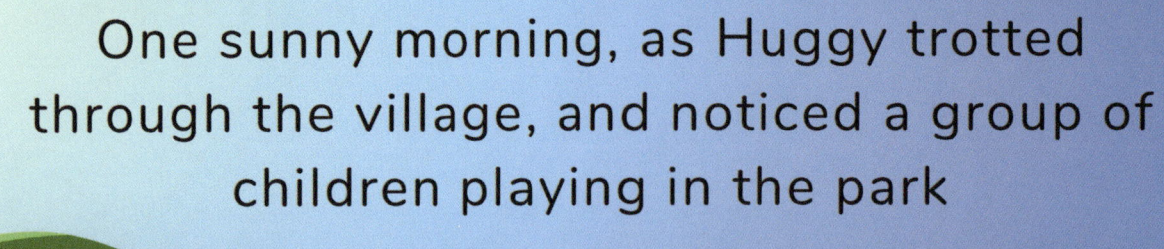

5 There was Lily, a shy girl who found it difficult to make friends.

and Alex, a boy who always seemed worried and anxious.

Huggy could sense their inner struggles and wanted to help them.

Huggy approached Lily and gently nuzzled her hand, letting her know that he understood her feelings.

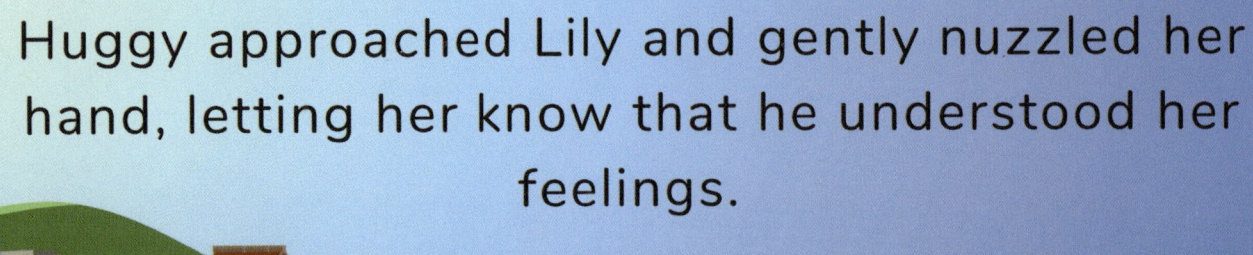

Lily's face lit up with a smile as she started to open up to Huggy. She shared her worries about starting a new school and making new friends.

7

Next, Huggy noticed Alex sitting alone on a bench, his arms folded and looking sad.

Huggy slowly made his way over and sat next to Alex.

Alex's worries started to fade away as he stroked Huggy's soft mane.

Huggy's presence brought a sense of calm to Alex's troubled mind. They talked about his fears and Huggy reassured him that it was okay to ask for help when needed.

Word quickly spread about Huggy's magical ability to provide comfort and support, and soon, teenagers and adults started seeking his therapy too.

Huggy created a safe space where people could share their thoughts and emotions without judgment.

As Huggy continued his therapy sessions, he realised that mental health was just as important as physical health.

He taught everyone the importance of caring for each other's well-being. Huggy encouraged kindness, empathy, and understanding in the village.

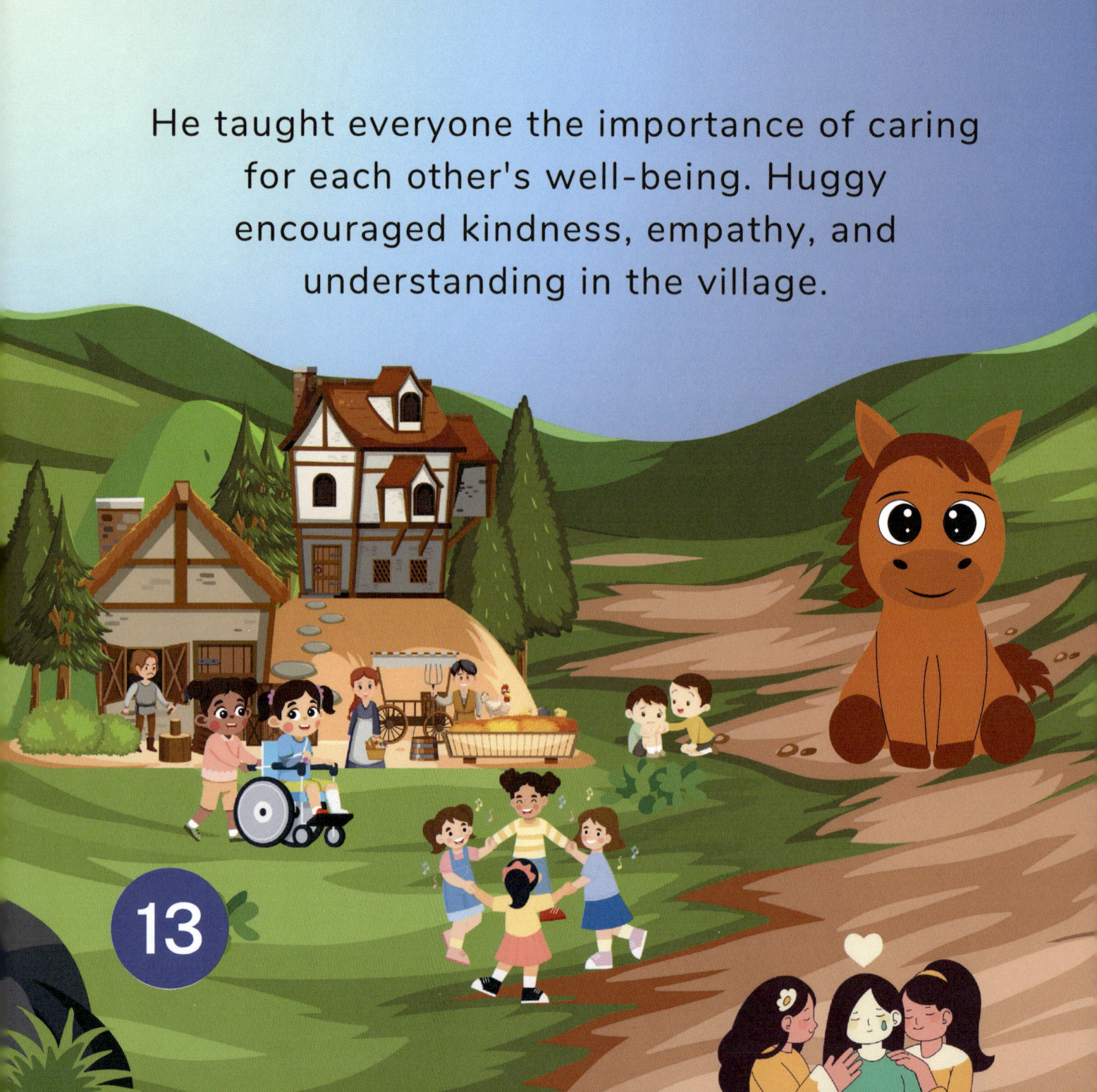

One day, the village decided to organise a Mental Health Awareness Day. They decorated the streets with colorful banners and held a parade, with Huggy leading the way.

Huggy's therapy sessions became even more popular after the event.

He continued to touch the lives of many, spreading love, compassion, and healing wherever he went.

Huggy proved that even the smallest of creatures could make a BIG difference in the world.

And so, the village lived happily ever after, with Huggy as a symbol of hope, friendship, and the importance of caring for each other's mental health.

HUGS OF ARGYLL

RAISING AWARENESS, ONE HUG AT A TIME

Info@hugsofargyll.com

www.hugsofargyll.com